D1017557

THE MESMER MENACE

— GADGETS AND GEARS —

THE MESMER MENACE

KERSTEN HAMILTON

with illustrations by

JAMES HAMILTON

CLARION BOOKS
Houghton Mifflin Harcourt
Boston   New York

CLARION BOOKS

215 Park Avenue South, New York, New York 10003

Clarion Books is an imprint of
Houghton Mifflin Harcourt Publishing Company.

The text of this book is set in Plantin.
The illustrations were executed digitally.
Design by Sharismar Rodriguez

www.hmhbooks.com

Library of Congress Cataloging-in-Publication Data
Hamilton, K. R. (Kersten R.)
The Mesmer menace / by Kersten Hamilton ; illustrated by James Hamilton.
pages cm. — ([Gadgets and gears ; book 1])
Summary: Daring dachshund Noodles narrates as evil Mesmers bent on world domination arrive at the Amazing Automated Inn, where eleven-year-old inventor Wally Kennewickett, aided by Noodles and the inn's automatons, tries to foil their plans.
ISBN 978-0-547-90568-6 (hardback)
[1. Adventure and adventurers—Fiction. 2. Dachshunds—Fiction.
3. Dogs—Fiction. 4. Hypnotism—Fiction. 5. Inventions—Fiction.
6. Robots—Fiction. 7. Humorous stories. 8. Science fiction.]
I. Hamilton, James (James Clayson), 1981–illustrator. II. Title.
PZ7.H1824Mes 2013   [Fic]—dc23
2012050257

Manufactured in the United States of America
DOC 10 9 8 7 6 5 4 3 2
4500451017

This is Sylvan's book.

—K.H.

anger.

I should have smelled it. Mayhem, most feathered and fowl, was coming.

I *should* have smelled it. But I didn't.

I smelled bacon and sausage, eggs and waffles, toast and tea—the scents we awoke to every morning at the Kennewicketts' Amazing Automated Inn.

My name is Noodles. I'm a dachshund.

On Saturday, October 19, 1902, the day the Great Mesmer War began, I was sitting on Wally Kennewickett's lap in the lobby as he perused the pages of an old *Scientific American*. Wally was reading an article about Percy Pilcher's last flight in his man-size glider the *Hawk*.

"Pilcher had built a *powered* plane, Noodles,"

Wally said, "but a mechanical malfunction forced him to fly the *Hawk* that fateful morning instead."

You learn a lot of interesting phrases living with the Kennewicketts. Phrases like *mechanical malfunction, retractable rail cannon,* and *flee for your life* were used quite frequently around the Inn.

"I wish they'd published Pilcher's blueprints for the powered plane!" Wally went on.

I licked his ear.

Manned, powered, and *controlled* flight in a contraption that was heavier than air was an achievement that had thus far eluded the world's most courageous adventurers and intelligent engineers. It was Wally Kennewickett's dream to be the first to achieve it. I did not approve. Flight was far too dangerous.

Percy Pilcher's perilous pursuit had ended when the *Hawk*'s tail failed and Percy plunged to his death. Wally took his journal from his pocket. He noted, *Tail failure may cause tragedy.*

I was pondering the profundity of this observation when destiny knocked on the door. Wally tucked his journal back in his pocket, set me on the couch, and stood up to answer it.

I barked.

"Jump, boy!" Wally said. "You can do it!"

My wagger went wild. It always does when Wally says "You can do it." But wagging wouldn't get me to the floor. There are things that nature never intended a dachshund to do. Flinging one-self off a couch is certainly on the list. I raced from one armrest to the other, barking madly until Wally came back and lifted me down. Wally Kennewickett is the kind of boy who comes through when you need him.

Once all four paws were safely on the pol-ished marble floor, I raced ahead of him to the door, expecting to find a Very Important Person on the steps. Scientists, businessmen, and engi-neers come to the Inn from all over the world, eager to ask for advice from Wally's parents, Oliver and Calypso Kennewickett.

Oliver and Calypso are *inventors extraordinaire*.

"Extraordinaire" means that they're amazing.

Oliver and Calypso invented everything in the Inn, from the Dust Bunnies to the Gyrating Generator and the Amazing Automatons. An "automaton" is a self-operating machine. The Kennewicketts are currently perfecting several new designs.

When Wally opened the door that morning, we didn't find a scientist, leader of industry, or engineer on the step, however. We found a hobo. The collar of his ragged coat was turned up, and the brim of his dusty hat was pulled down. I could just make out a bulb of a nose above a bushy mustache, and perhaps the flash of spectacles.

"Walter Kennewickett," the hobo said, "I must see your parents at once. It's a matter of utmost importance!"

It wasn't surprising that a hobo would know Wally's name. The Kennewicketts were always kind to hobos.

"Yes, sir," Wally said politely. "Would you wait in the lobby while I find them?"

"Of course." The hobo looked at me. "Is this fine fellow your dog?"

"My best friend," Wally corrected. "His name is Noodles. I'll return shortly, sir."

I wanted to follow Wally, but felt it might be best if I waited with our guest. The Automated Inn is conveniently located near a branch of the Union Pacific Railroad, so I had observed many hobos. Some of them were nice, ordinary people. Others put things in their pockets when no one was watching. If our visitor was that sort of hobo, he would soon find out that dachshunds are very good at watching.

This hobo didn't try to slip anything in his pockets. He patted my head, then walked to the fireplace to ponder the portrait of a pigeon that hung above the mantel. Half of the Kennewickett clan have a particular passion for the birds. Wally's almost-grown-up cousin Melvin Kennewickett has a shelf full of pigeon racing trophies. Melvin's twin sister, Prissy, has half a shelf of trophies. They'd inherited this peculiar pastime from their father, Wentworth Kennewickett, who, being Oliver's elder brother, technically owned the Inn. But it hadn't been an inn when he'd left it in Oliver's care, and it certainly had not been automated.

It had been a frightening folly built atop a granite mountain by Oliver and Wentworth's industrialist grandfather, the wicked Mars Kennewickett. Kennewicketts tend to turn out generally good or abominably evil. Oliver keeps a journal of his own,

full of notes, observations, and theories about this family phenomenon.

Wally worries about it. Sometimes I find him in front of the full-length mirror on Calypso's side of the lab, staring into his own green eyes. I know what he is thinking. He is pondering the conundrum of his kin: Which sort of Kennewickett am *I* going to be?

A "conundrum" is a difficult problem or question. The kind Kennewicketts love best.

Wally's father is the generally good sort of Kennewickett. At least, he has been since he married Wally's mother. It was Calypso who had insisted that the cannons be removed from the folly's turret, and the chains taken out of the dungeons Mars had dug into the solid stone of the mountain.

I felt this had been a step in the right direction. Letting Melvin, Prissy, and their pigeons stay, however, was a step in the wrong direction, even if their father did technically own the Inn.

The pigeons' presence gave Wally an excuse

to spend too much time locked away with his gadgets and gears. Wally is allergic to feathers.

The hobo rubbed his chin, and I realized my mind had wandered far from the issue at hand. *Was this the kind of hobo who would slip things into his pocket?* I had just decided that he was the ordinary, honest sort when I noticed his boots. They were shiny beneath a thin film of dust— too shiny. The cuffs of his trousers weren't torn, either. *He's wearing a disguise,* I thought.

"Are you a pigeon fancier, sir?" asked Oliver Kennewickett, stepping into the room. Wally and Calypso were right behind him. Walter Kennewickett does not look like either of his parents. Oliver is tall and dark, with flashing black eyes; Calypso is fair and elegant in every way. Wally is small for his age, and his hair is the color of new copper wire.

"A pigeon fancier?" the hobo said, turning around. "Not in the least."

I had to wag. Pigeons engage in activities such as flying, eating bugs, and perching on high places. You'd never catch a dachshund doing such senseless things.

"How can we help you?" asked Calypso Kennewickett kindly. "Breakfast, perhaps? A hot bath?"

"We've no time for that," the hobo said. He took off his coat and hat.

Wally gasped. *"Theodore Roosevelt!"*

"Mr. President!" Oliver Kennewickett exclaimed. "What an unexpected honor!"

2

I came in utmost secrecy," the president said.

"But how, sir?" Oliver asked. "And why?"

I was wondering that myself.

"By unmarked coach to the town in the valley below, then onward by foot," Mr. Roosevelt explained.

"But surely your coach could have dropped you at our door?" Calypso queried.

There were just two ways to get to our inn, which occupies a ledge high above the lovely town of Gasket Gully. You could come up the elevator Oliver had installed, which carries visitors from the train station to the cliff top, then have a pleasant stroll across the lawn to the front door, or you could risk the harrowing road that

Mad Mars's cannons had once looked over. Hobos most often made their way up the road.

"I feared an official trip might draw unwanted attention." The president looked grim. "I need to speak to you before I risk summoning my coach. Is there somewhere safe we can converse?"

Calypso pulled the bell cord, and Gizmo stepped out of a secret door in the wall. Gizmo is Oliver and Calypso's most amazing invention. She may look like a pleasant maid in a multi-pocketed apron, clockwork corset, and button boots, but Gizmo's mind is more than the sum of its cogs and wheels. It's packed with facts, diagrams for silly things like dirigibles, and useful things such as prize-winning cookie recipes. Gizmo is the housekeeper, governess, cook, and scientific assistant at the Automated Inn. Like our other large automatons, Gizmo is electrical. Her charging closet is cunningly concealed in the lobby, so she's always on hand.

"We'll take tea in the private parlor, Gizmo," Calypso said.

"Right away, madam," Gizmo replied.

"Ahem." The president looked pointedly at Walter. "I'm afraid we have a very delicate matter to discuss."

"We keep no secrets from our son," Oliver Kennewickett said.

"He is a scientist in training," Calypso explained. "Hair, Walter!" Calypso believes that untidiness is an indication of a messy mind. She thinks the most important question a scientist can ask is "Is this experiment elegant?" Which is why Calypso's side of the lab is meticulously kept.

Oliver produced a pocket comb and handed it to his son. Oliver believes that one should be prepared for every possibility. He thinks the most important question a scientist can ask is "What if?" Which is why Oliver's pockets are always full of interesting and useful things.

President Roosevelt looked from Calypso to Oliver, then nodded.

Wally tidied his hair as we stepped into the private parlor.

No one questioned whether or not *I* should come along, of course. Dachshunds are known for their discretion and their keen attendance to duty.

Which is why, when I saw a Dust Bunny peeking out from behind a chair, I chased it across the carpet and under the couch before the president noticed. The job of Calypso's clockwork Dust Bunnies is cleaning the floors, bookshelves, and tabletops. They are supposed to hide when we have guests.

It's my job to help them remember that.

When I came out from under the couch, Mr. Roosevelt was standing, hands behind his back, staring out the wall-size parlor window. Oliver, Calypso, and Wally sat politely, waiting for him to speak.

I walked over to see what he was looking at. Visitors always comment on the excellent view from this window. We could see Theoden McDivit pedaling his velocipede down Grommet Street far below in Gasket Gully. In the distance, past the rooftops of the town, the train trestle hung suspended high above the churning waters of the mighty Oblivion River.

The president paced to the window at the far side of the room. The view from this one was not so nice. On the small lawn outside, Melvin was showing his pigeon coop to a rotund gentleman in a top hat. Even from behind, I recognized Mortimer McDivit, the mayor of Gasket Gully. Melvin has political aspirations.

That means he intends to run for office himself one day. In Melvin's case, it also means that he is much more likely to be nice to you if he thinks you are a Very Important Person.

Behind them, Prissy was attempting to teach

her birds tumbling tricks. She had recently attended a circus and was contemplating life under the Big Top.

"Are these your older children?" inquired Mr. Roosevelt. "Should we ask them in as well?"

"Our niece and nephew," Calypso said. "And whether we should ask them in is a delicate question. Perhaps we should wait until we have heard your dilemma before we decide if they should be told."

I agreed. Prissy Kennewickett cannot keep secrets. She never slips me scraps off the table, either. Melvin only gives me the things he doesn't want to eat himself, like carrots or cabbage. Their annoying birds live on the lawn so that they won't make a mess of Oliver's experiments on the roof.

Mr. Roosevelt watched Prissy do a somersault, then nodded thoughtfully and turned to survey the room.

I saw the Dust Bunny zip out from under the couch just as Gizmo entered with the tea and cookies. I was across the room in a flash.

The Dust Bunny skittered between Gizmo's feet. Before I could get past the ambulatory automaton, the dastardly Dust Bunny had climbed up Calypso's skirt and hidden in her pocket.

President Roosevelt took a seat.

"The country needs your amazing brains, Kennewicketts," he said as Gizmo filled his cup. "Our agents have uncovered the tracks of an unscrupulous organization."

"An organization of evil scientists?" Wally asked hopefully.

I growled. We had recently been reading an excellent book by Mr. Jules Verne that was full of evil scientists.

"An organization of"—Mr. Roosevelt put his teacup down—*"magicians."*

Wally picked me up and I settled beside him.

"Magicians?" Calypso offered the president a

cookie. "The kind with capes, canes, and hats?"

"Precisely," he said, choosing a macaroon. "They call themselves the Mesmers, and we fear that they plan to take over the world."

"Through the use of stage tricks and skullduggery?" Oliver asked.

"Through the use of *mind control*," the president said grimly.

Wally gasped.

"The name 'Mesmer' may be a reference to physician Franz Mesmer, 1734 to 1815," said Gizmo. "Mesmer claimed to practice animal magnetism."

"Of course," Oliver said. "Mesmer's theories led to the development of hypnotism!"

"Precisely," the president agreed. "The danger, I fear, is real. The Mesmers are targeting leaders of government, industry, and finance, confounding and controlling their minds. We've kept it quiet, but news stories are beginning to appear—such as the tale of the pasha who leaped from a clock tower flapping his arms as if he could fly."

A "pasha" is an official of the Ottoman Empire. Pashas, princes, and prime ministers were all frequent visitors at the Inn. Most of them seemed far too sensible to attempt flight.

Theodore Roosevelt grimaced. "Edith—I mean, my wife—fears they might mesmerize me. Imagine the president of the United States a puppet to some evil power."

"The fiends!" Wally jumped out of his seat, nearly toppling me from the chair. "They must be foiled!"

C orrect," the president concurred. "I'm here to ask your parents to become agents of the U.S. government, Walter!"

If Theodore Roosevelt had not been the president, I thought he would have made an excellent agent himself. Everyone knew he had the courage of a corsair and practiced the oriental art of judo in the hallowed halls of the White House.

"Sit down, Walter," Calypso said. "I believe we need to hear more before any decisions are made."

"Of course, Mother," Wally said, flushing. He sat down and I crawled onto his lap.

Our noble leader tapped his nose. "The agent bit must be hush-hush, of course."

"Why us?" Oliver asked.

"Who better to expose tricks and skullduggery than our nation's top scientists?" said Mr. Roosevelt. "I feel you will be able to figure out how they are confounding minds in the Kremlin and eliminating leaders of the Ottoman Empire before they bring confusion to our own capital!"

"Interesting." Calypso selected a cookie. "I've always felt I would excel at espionage."

"Espionage" is gathering information that other people don't want you to have. It's what secret agents and spies do.

"I'm sure you would, dear," Oliver said. "*I've* certainly never managed to keep anything from you. But isn't this a job for the Secret Service? Or perhaps the Pinkertons?"

The employees of the Pinkerton National Detective Agency are fearless fellows who spend their time pursuing evildoers.

"I am in the midst of a rather important experiment, Mr. President," Oliver explained.

"My husband is collaborating with Nikola Tesla," Calypso said, "in an experiment that may make free and abundant electric power available to the entire world!"

"Tesla is a brilliant man," the president admitted. "I follow his experiments."

"Then you may be interested in a small demonstration." Oliver stood up. "Gizmo!"

Gizmo stepped to the corner and unveiled a model of the Automated Inn, complete with sail-like lightning collectors next to the Gyrating Generator on top.

"Everything is readied." Oliver circumnavigated the room, scuffing his boots on Calypso's fine Persian rug. "And my equipment predicts an electrical disturbance in the atmosphere within three days!"

"You mean a lightning storm carrying a charge such as your boot soles are gathering from the carpet," the president guessed shrewdly. "Your Inn is positioned perfectly to collect atmospheric electrons at this altitude!"

I was impressed with our president yet again. Oliver's atmospheric experiments *are* aided by the fact that the Automated Inn is perched high on a precipice, even if it means we are far above such modern conveniences as telegraph wires.

"Oliver hopes to transmit power," Calypso said, "over a thousand miles through the earth to a waiting receptor at Tesla's Colorado Springs Experimental Station."

"Here represented," Oliver pointed, "by the minuscule amount of flash powder my assistant has just deposited on the opposite side of the room."

Gizmo backed away from the smidgen of powder she had poured onto a tray. I hid my nose under Wally's arm.

Oliver went on, "Both the collector on the model and the receptor on the tray are connected to the solid marble floor beneath this rug—"

"Which in this case represents the earth's crust!" declared the president, leaping to his feet in the excitement of the moment.

Oliver held his finger over the model of the Inn and a spark leaped from his fingertip to the electron collectors on top. Instantly the flash powder on the opposite side of the room exploded in light.

"Bravo!" President Roosevelt waved away the subsequent smoke. "You've blown up Tesla's lab!"

"That was merely for visual effect, sir," said Gizmo. "No actual labs will be harmed in the experiment."

"At least, not if all goes as planned," added Calypso. "Though Oliver does love a good explosion."

"Don't we all?" Mr. Roosevelt exclaimed as they settled into their seats once more. "It's brilliant, of course. And yet difficult choices must be made. Your country is in danger, Kennewicketts!"

"Oliver's point, Mr. President," Calypso interjected, "is that science is not something one can simply walk away from. Each experiment takes planning and preparation. Asking him to leave just now is like asking a farmer to abandon his fields just as his crops are ready to be harvested. It would be wasting an entire year of preparation."

"Calypso is expecting a trainload of guests tomorrow as well," Oliver added. "A convention of popcorn vendors and Professor Potts, the world's foremost expert on the cultivation and popping of corn."

Calypso's practical inventions not only made the world a better place; they also provided the Kennewicketts with funding for further scientific research.

"We are expecting nineteen vendors," said Calypso. "They are interested in my newly developed Lightning-Fast Popcorn Popper, Suitable for Spectacles and Special Events. Potts will be presenting a series of talks, and I have promised a demonstration of the device."

Mr. Roosevelt looked from Oliver to Calypso. I could tell he was thinking that they were an amazing team.

"Perhaps we could wait to become agents?" Oliver suggested. "Just for a few days, until the convention is over and the storm has passed?"

Everyone was silent for a heartbeat, and then Wally stood up again, still holding me tight.

"Is there something you'd like to say, Walter?" Calypso asked.

"Yes, Mother." Wally's face flushed. "I feel that protecting the president is our higher duty. *I* can observe and record Father's data."

I wagged my tail. Wally is very responsible when he isn't inventing.

"You can count on me as well, master and madam," Gizmo said. "I am wired for patriotism."

This sounded promising. Gizmo often ran the Inn while the Kennewicketts were away on scientific expeditions. We did have an excellent, if automated, staff.

"Mr. Jones will be stopping by as well," Gizmo went on. "He can assist if there is anything amiss with the machinery."

I wagged *and* wiggled. Mr. Jones is the exceptional engineer who drives the train to Kennewickett Station. He's practically part of the family. Mr. Jones and Gizmo share blueprints and secret cookie recipes; he and Oliver share intelligence and occasional conspiracy theories.

Calypso says that if Mr. Jones wrote novels, he'd be better than Mr. Verne.

Oliver says the fact that Mr. Jones has never once been right doesn't mean he never will be.

I say that Mr. Jones is an outstanding friend.

He would certainly lend assistance if any device needed mending in Oliver and Calypso's absence. And he makes superb snickerdoodles.

Oliver nodded. "I applaud your sentiments, son," he said slowly. "And yours as well, Gizmo. I don't like the sound of these menacing Mesmers either. Still, this is a difficult decision. Son, would you take Mr. Roosevelt on a tour while your mother, Gizmo, and I discuss this development?"

"Bully!" the president said, by which he meant *Splendid! I'd love a tour!*

"Walter," Calypso said as we reached the door, "let's not discuss the menace outside this room."

"Yes, Mother," said Wally as he motioned for me and the president to step into the hallway, and pulled the door shut behind us.

W e paused in the lobby to allow the president to don his disguise. You never know whom you might meet in the hallways of the Inn. Because it has forty-two rooms on three floors (not counting the dungeons or the turret), three libraries, and several conservatories and cozy parlors, it is possible to overlook a quiet chemist intent on his research, or a monk meditating in a corner.

The president was pulling down his hat brim when Melvin and Prissy came in. The mayor must have made his way back to town, because he wasn't with them. Prissy was carrying a pigeon, however. The creatures, coop and all, had arrived by coach along with Wally's cousins and their boxes and trunks just two months before.

"May I present Melvin and Priscill*ah-ah-ah-choo!*" Wally sneezed. "*Please* leave the pigeons outside, Priss. You know Mother doesn't allow them in the house. And I've told you I am *ah-choo!*" Wally rubbed his nose. "I meant *allergic,* of course."

"And we've told you that Columbidae are nothing to sneeze at!" Melvin insists on referring to pigeons by their scientific family name. He *is* a Kennewickett, after all. The question is, what kind of Kennewickett? Oliver has whole subsections in his journal dedicated to Melvin and Prissy. If he knew half of what they were up to, there would be reams more. But Wally believes that scientists in training should never be tattletales.

I could feel a growl growing inside me. Melvin calls Wally "runt" or "nincompoop" when he thinks no one else can hear. Someone should tell Melvin that dachshunds have excellent ears, and a very good understanding of slang. A "runt" is someone who is smaller than he should be. "Nincompoop" means a stupid or foolish person. Wally is small, but he is *never* foolish.

And if someone were to talk to Wally's cousins, they might also mention to Prissy that dachshunds are not unskilled in the art of deduction. When I see her sneaking out of Wally's room and later find a feather folded into his pillowslip, it is simplicity itself to deduce *exactly* how it got there.

Wally pretends his cousins' cutting comments and cruel jests don't concern him. He also tries to pretend that scientists in training don't cry. Wally isn't very good at pretending. At least not late at night when all the lights are off and his parents are fast asleep.

My theory is that Melvin and Prissy have far too much of Mars Kennewickett in them—but President

Roosevelt couldn't be expected to know that. He tried to be pleasant to the rotters.

"Pleased to meet you," he said. "I understand that you are Walter's cousins?"

"Precisely," Prissy said primly.

"Are your parents living at the Inn?"

"We're orphans," Melvin offered.

Wally winced. I shook my ears. Melvin 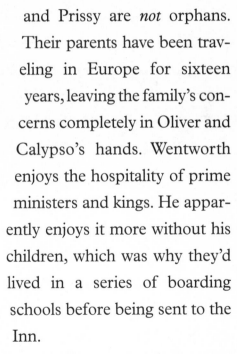 and Prissy are *not* orphans. Their parents have been traveling in Europe for sixteen years, leaving the family's concerns completely in Oliver and Calypso's hands. Wentworth enjoys the hospitality of prime ministers and kings. He apparently enjoys it more without his children, which was why they'd lived in a series of boarding schools before being sent to the Inn.

Oliver insists that even pretend orphans often turn

out better than expected if they are given a chance. But he had also insisted that Jeeves, his first attempt at an automated lab assistant, would not go mad and use his retractable rail cannon to try to take over the world. The desire to rule the world appears to be the first symptom of a malfunctioning mind.

"If you must befriend hobos, Walter," Prissy whispered loudly, "you should do so outside. I'm sure they are much nastier than pigeons."

"Quite right," Melvin said. "Remove this dusty . . . *person* . . . immediately. Kennewick-etts do not consort with the riff and raff of this world, Walter! Ow!" Melvin grabbed his ankle. He didn't have to hop and howl in such an un-dignified manner. I hadn't nipped him *that* hard.

"I'm positive my parents would not approve of removing him," Wally said. "In fact, I have been instructed to give Mr.—"

"TR." Mr. Roosevelt put his hand on Wally's shoulder. His spectacles flashed. "Call me TR, son."

"I have been instructed to give *TR* a tour,"

Wally said, pinking slightly at the deception. It is possible that Wally would not make a very good spy.

"Then tour somewhere far away from us," Priscilla said.

"Right-o!" The president winked at Walter. "We will stay away. Shall we go, Walter?"

"An automaton infestation, vicious dogs, and *hobos*," Melvin said as Wally walked away. "What next?"

"There are Kennewicketts, and then there are *Kennewicketts*," Prissy said, stroking her pigeon's head. "Changes may need to be made."

5

Dust Bunnies peeked at us from every crack and crevice as we went down the stone stairs to the dungeons, where the Kennewicketts' famous laboratory is located. Calypso feels that keeping experiments in the subterranean regions is safer for the guests.

Mr. Tesla had almost leaped with joy when he'd visited the lab. The Automated Inn was the only facility on the planet that perfectly met his needs: the rooftop scraped the clouds, and the dungeons bored into the very core of the mountain.

"It is necessary for the machine to get a grip of

the earth," the great inventor had explained, running his hand along the cold stone. "A grip so deep that the whole of this globe can quiver!"

Mad Mars's delving into the mountain had apparently made this "gripping the earth" possible.

When we reached the deepest level, Wally helped me into my lab coat and goggles.

"Science can be a perilous pursuit," he explained as he handed the president a lab coat to replace his hobo disguise.

"Quite a lot of storage here," the president observed, patting the sides of his coat.

"Mother designed them," Wally said proudly. "Father and I both find a plethora of pockets useful in the lab."

When Wally had donned his own gear, he pulled a lever and the giant doors swung wide.

"Magnificent," the president murmured as he stepped inside.

Golden spheres hung in the air, spinning soundlessly. Arcs of blue electricity climbed ladder-like between giant posts. Copper fly-wheels moved cranks and shafts that led into the stone walls. We were surrounded by amazing mechanical apparatus, but if you looked closely you could see that the lab was roughly divided, with one half reflecting Oliver's interests and the other half Calypso's.

Nestled among the electrical contraptions on Oliver's side lurked the instruments of an ancient alchemist. Glittering curlicues of glass carried colored condensation from bubbling beakers. A small steam engine of ancient Greek design chuffed and rattled on the countertop.

In contrast, Calypso's collection of advanced Analytical Engines, drafting tables, mannequins, and a well-sorted selection of millinery looked completely modern. I met Jeeves's eye in her full-length modeling mirror.

The ex-butler's head peered in a most unnerving fashion from amid the pile of parts under Wally's workbench, which was situated

comfortably between the workspaces of his parents.

I couldn't help but wish someone had removed Jeeves's malfunctioning mechanism from the jumble of junk, but the president probably wouldn't see his unsettling stare. Not unless he sat down on the floor.

"What's all this?" the president asked, examining the bin full of broken bits of wood, scraps of colored silk, wire umbrella ribs, rubber wheels, and kite tails on top of Wally's workspace.

"Failed flying machines," Wally admitted. "I have been trying to piece together the puzzle of powered controlled flight."

"Failed?"

"I have tried a thousand times," Wally said sadly. "I fear it is time to give up."

I thought this was a very good idea. The world needed many things, but powered controlled flight was not one of them. Unfortunately, Theodore Roosevelt did not agree.

"Give up!" he boomed. "Never say so, Walter! The boy who is going to make a great man must not make up his mind merely to overcome a thousand obstacles, but to *win* in spite of a thousand repulses and defeats!"

"Do you mind if I write that down?" Wally asked, taking his journal from his pocket.

"Not at all," the president replied. He was apparently accustomed to being inspiring.

I kept a close eye on Wally as he wrote. If he was suddenly struck by inspiration, he might forget the Mesmers, the tour, and even the president himself. I frequently had to save Wally from disaster when he was caught up in a scientific conundrum. Once, I'd caught his coattail *seconds* before he was about to step into an empty elevator shaft. Fortunately, no fantastical idea formed in Wally's mind as he focused on his note.

The president leaned over a vat of trapped lightning. He tapped the side, causing miniature bolts to arc inside the glass, searching for a way out.

"Is your mother's Lightning-Fast Popcorn Popper actually powered by the lightning your father collects?"

"Yes, sir." Wally tucked his notebook back into his pocket. "If the vendors buy machines, they will also order lightning bolts with which to power them. Father has collected an ample supply."

"And how do you transfer the lightning to the popping machine?"

Wally pulled on his gauntlets, opened the vat, and grabbed a bolt.

"Good Gad!" the president said. I felt this must be an exclamation of admiration for Wally's hair.

"Errant electrons," Wally explained, carefully drawing the miniature bolt out of the vat.

"Errant" means wandering in search of adventure. There are always a few errant electrons in the air, and they are generally attracted to Wally's head. When lightning plays across the Atmospheric Electron Collectors on the roof

and sizzles down the wires to the Voltage Vats, Prissy claims Wally resembles a mad scientist.

"It takes one miniature bolt to power the popper. Father's device splits lightning bolts into smaller units such as this." Wally transferred the bolt to a jar. "We mustn't waste any. The electrons in the vats are for mother's Lightning-Fast

Popcorn Popper demonstration. Father has diverted the power lines in order to transmit the next lightning bolt he collects to Mr. Tesla's lab."

The president polished his spectacles, and then peered into the gloomy recesses of the lab where the cable branched at a giant switch. One tree-trunk-size bundle of wires snaked toward the Voltage Vats; the other led to a huge copper coil and Oliver's transmission device.

"The whole Inn doesn't run on electrons harvested from storms, then?" the president asked.

"Lightning stored in these vats was once used for the Inn," Wally said, setting the jar on a shelf. "My parents found electrical storms too unpredictable to power the daily workings of multiple automatons."

I was glad he did not mention that Jeeves's malfunction came about after a particularly powerful lightning storm had supercharged his wiring.

"But the wind *always* blows here," Wally went on, "which allows our Gyrating Generator to produce the regular electron flow we need."

"The spinning contraption on top of the model Inn? Can I get a look at the real McCoy?"

I shivered. "The real McCoy" means "the real thing," or "the genuine article." Mr. Roosevelt was suggesting an excursion to the roof.

"Certainly," Wally said. "We'd best keep our lab coats on, sir. Mother insists on it around any experimental equipment."

6

I may have mentioned that dachshunds do not like heights? But if Walter Kennewickett was going to the rooftops, I was going too. My lab coat would have to hide my trembling. I collected my courage and followed Wally up flight after flight of stairs.

When we reached the roof, the wind whipped my ears as Wally and the president started up the long ladder that clung to the side of the turret. Thankfully, it was completely impossible for me to follow. Dachshunds do not navigate ladders. Wally's canvas coattails flapped like a flag as he climbed. Watching him made my head spin and my stomach feel light, as if gravity were turning topsy-turvy and at any moment my paws might lose their grip and I would fall *up* into the wide

blue sky and tumble away forever. I
tucked my tail and covered my goggles with my paws.

When Wally returned at last
from the terrible blue abyss, I
could not contain my joy.

"Look at that wagger go!"
said President Roosevelt.
"If it were a propeller, the
fellow'd be a proper whirligig!"

Wally picked me up,
and I licked his chin all
the way down the stairs.

When we reached
the lab, we retired our
coats and goggles and
the president donned
his disguise once more.
Then we returned to
the comfort of the lobby.
The door to the private
parlor was still closed.

"That was a bully tour!" Theodore Roosevelt said, which meant he thought that Wally had done a very good job. "You answered my every question, Walter. Is there anything you would like to ask me? Aside from questions about the you-know-whos, of course."

Wally hesitated.

"Out with it, son!" the president said. "What would you like to know?"

"I have long been curious about the oriental art of—"

"Judo!" the president exclaimed, assuming a fighting stance. "Some things must be demonstrated, not discussed!" He expertly executed seven effective combat stances and one keen judo throw, then let Wally have a go.

The door to the private parlor opened.

"Mr. and Mrs. Kennewickett will see you now," Gizmo announced as Wally helped the president to his feet. Wally is small, but he excels at sports.

Calypso and Oliver were both standing when we entered the room.

"Hair, Walter!" Calypso said. Everyone looked discreetly away as Wally quickly combed down his electrified locks.

"We have concluded that our son is correct," Oliver announced when Wally was in order again. "Sometimes citizenship requires sacrifice. We must do what we can."

"It is our duty as citizens to protect the president," Calypso added, "and as intelligent beings to save the world! Walter will watch over the experiments for his father, and Gizmo will run the convention."

"Well done, Walter!" the president said. "My coach will arrive in thirty minutes."

"So quickly?" Calypso asked.

"I signaled my Secret Service men from the

top of the turret. We must move fast. The Mesmers may be scheming even as we speak!"

"There is no point in our assuming disguises, I assume?" Oliver looked hopefully at the president's hobo gear.

"None," Calypso decreed. "Our standing in the scientific community will offer the cover we need."

It was true that the Kennewicketts were often out and about in odd company.

"It goes without saying," Oliver said, "that no magicians of any sort should be admitted to the Inn in our absence."

"Of course not, Father," Wally agreed.

"Summon Melvin and Prissy, Gizmo," instructed Calypso. "And assemble the staff. We mustn't leave without saying goodbye. I'll compose a note for Professor Potts."

Half an hour later, the staff and family were assembled in the lobby of the Inn. Gizmo had not only summoned the staff but also prepared a picnic breakfast for the travelers to take along.

7

Calypso had dressed stylishly as always, with a map case and brass spyglass by her side. Oliver's jacket and boots gave him a piratical air, belied only by the handsome top hat and assortment of tools, fobs, and plumb bobs that hung from his pockets and belt.

In short, they were as elegant and well prepared as ever. I walked proudly beside them as they surveyed the staff.

Knives, the silent assistant cook whose multiple bladed attachments allow him to slice, dice, chop, and puree at incredible speeds, stood at attention on one side of Gizmo. Talos, the towering bronze footman who had assumed many of the butler's duties after the unfortunate incident with Jeeves, stood on the other. The maids and kitchen help were arrayed behind them. I felt the elder Kennewicketts could be confident leaving the Inn in the hands of such a competent crew.

Oliver gave them a few last-moment instructions, while Calypso hugged Melvin, then Prissy.

"But *why* are you hurrying off with this hobo?" Prissy whined.

"We can't tell you that just yet, dear." Calypso plucked a feather from Prissy's sleeve before Wally could catch wind of it. "But we hope to reveal all when we return. In the meantime, please provide Gizmo with any help she requires."

I wished, and not for the first time, that I had the power of human speech. If the elder Kennewicketts knew what rotters Melvin and Prissy were, they'd lock them in their respective rooms until they returned. But they didn't.

"Take care of the coops, Melvin," Oliver instructed instead.

"Right-o," Melvin said.

"Remember to oil the other automatons, Gizmo," Calypso added. "And don't forget to wind the Dust Bunnies. We wouldn't want the

Inn to be untidy." Dust Bunnies are a great deal of trouble. They must be wound once a day or they simply cease to dust.

"Give my regrets to Mr. Jones, Walter," Oliver said. "We will miss our meeting. And remember to record the readings both before and after the storm."

Calypso kissed Wally's cheek and smoothed his hair, which had started to stand up again.

"I expect you will look after my atmospheric experiments admirably, son." Oliver offered his hand.

I could see that the thought of his parents going off to save the world without him was difficult for Wally, for he swallowed hard before he shook his father's hand.

"Yes, sir. I will."

"Noodles!" Oliver nodded when he saw me sitting up, ready for my instructions. "Take care of Wally for us."

It pleased me that Oliver and Calypso knew I didn't need to be told to keep the Dust Bunnies in line. Dachshunds are always on the job!

"We'll return as soon as we are able." Calypso straightened the crimson lace of her parasol. "Until then, we are depending on you all to keep the Inn in tiptop form."

I heard the rattle of carriage wheels on the drive. Talos picked up the Kennewicketts' bags, and Gizmo dismissed the staff.

Melvin and Prissy were conspiring in the corner when Wally stepped up to the hobo.

"It was a great honor meeting you, sir," he said.

"And you as well, Walter. Remember . . ." The hobo tapped his nose.

"The secret's safe with me, sir," Wally whispered.

"We'll be on the road," the hobo whispered back, "but if you need to get in touch, the missus might know where I am. Remember what I told you, Walter. Never give up!"

Wally pressed his hand to the pocket that held the notebook in which he'd recorded the president's words.

"Never, sir!"

Theodore Roosevelt winked, and then they were gone.

I started for the dining room. Breakfast had been delayed so long, it had become brunch. I was halfway down the hall when I realized Wally wasn't with me. I raced back and found him standing in front of Melvin with a most peculiar look on his face.

"Walter," Melvin said, "stop staring!"

Wally appeared to be gazing at Melvin, but I knew he wasn't seeing him. I may have mentioned that Walter Kennewickett gets caught up in conundrums?

I had overheard Oliver and Calypso discussing this dilemma the day I'd saved Wally from stepping into the elevator shaft.

Calypso had been concerned over his seeming inattention to details such as open pits, or people addressing him directly. Oliver had pointed out that one of their young German friends, Albert Einstein, often exhibited the same tendencies. He was certain both Wally and Albert would overcome their absent-mindedness to become great scientists one day.

"Why does he have that expression on his face, Mel?" Prissy asked. "He looks like a complete nincompoop."

"Well?" Melvin demanded. "What do you have to say for yourself, Walter? Why the foolish face?"

"Whirligig!" Wally said happily. The word filled me with a strange foreboding.

"Well, we have something to say to you." Melvin moved closer. "Real Kennewicketts have no tolerance for nincompoopery! While your parents are traveling with that tramp, *stay away from us.*"

I thought that was a top-notch idea. I took Wally's pants cuff in my teeth and tugged him toward the dining room.

Wally was too focused on the diagrams he was drawing in his gravy to eat.

"Not right," he muttered as I finished his last sausage. "Not quite. But with a slight modification . . . Yes!" He put his fork down. "Noodles! To the lab!"

Excellent. The lab was far away from Melvin and Prissy.

Once we were there, Wally went to work, stopping only to pace and mutter about "overcoming a thousand obstacles." When he figured out some particularly puzzling problem, he would run his hand through his hair and laugh before rushing back to his bench.

I yawned. Certain scientific moments are not exactly the stuff excitement is made of. Fortunately, the lab was well equipped for napping dachshunds. I found my pillow in the corner, turned my back on Jeeves's baleful gaze, and drifted off.

Wally's hair was all standing on end when he woke me in order to demonstrate his invention.

"It is finished, Noodles," he said, holding up a small vest with bat-like folding wings.

I tried to shake the sleep out of my ears as he buttoned me into it.

"You're amazing!" Wally said.

I wagged. Even a sleepy tail *must* respond when Wally says that. The wings flapped up and down.

"You can do it, boy!"

My wagger went wild.

Suddenly, I came fully awake to find that *I'd risen to the ceiling*. My fear of falling into the air had come true. All that saved me from tumbling into the frightening blue firmament was the stone ceiling.

My tail froze, and for one horrifying instant I knew how Pilcher must have felt during the first moment of his fatal fall.

Tail failure may cause tragedy . . . !

. . . And then Wally caught me.

"Mr. Roosevelt was right!" Wally said happily. "You *are* practically as good as a whirligig, Noodles! Who should we show first? Gizmo? No! We'll wait for Mr. Jones and show them together!"

I checked my tail. It wasn't wagging. I didn't know if it would ever wag again. Wally took the unnerving vest off me and tucked it into one of his many pockets.

I didn't sleep a wink that night. I lay awake, staring at the ceiling but seeing in my mind's eye the terrifying starry expanse beyond.

8

When the steam engine puffed into Kennewickett Station at the foot of the mountain the next day, Prissy, Melvin, Wally, and I were gathered on the platform to greet the guests. By "gathered" I mean that Prissy and Melvin were standing as far from Wally as they possibly could.

My heart was as heavy as my eyelids, because I knew I was going to let Wally down. It was as if my tail had a mind of its own, a mind that could not ignore the coming catastrophe. It had not wagged once all morning. Not once.

Mr. Jones leaped from the locomotive as the popcorn vendors poured off the train. My keen nose could find him even in the buttery-sweet-smelling sea of candy-striped coats, bamboo canes, and straw boater hats. Mr. Jones smells of soot and cinders, and his pockets are always full of spicy snickerdoodles. He's the only human I've ever known who can carry more tools about his person than Oliver Kennewickett. This is because there is so much more of Mr. Jones from which to hang useful items.

"'Ello, Noodles!" he boomed as he tossed me one of his famous snickerdoodles. Not even a depressed dachshund could resist such a treat.

"Is your father at the Inn, Walter?" Mr. Jones asked as Melvin and Prissy led the guests to the elevator that would carry them up the cliff.

"I'm afraid he's away," Wally said.

"Away?" Mr. Jones asked, eyeing a dapper dandy who lagged behind the crowd of passengers.

"On business," Wally explained. "But I have something important to show you, sir. An invention of my own!"

I sat down on my tail. It was as if disaster was rushing at me, and I had no way to elude it.

Wally was going to ask me to fly, and I *could not* do it. Not again. I was doomed to fail Wally in his moment of greatest achievement.

"Excellent!" Mr. Jones said, glancing at his pocket chronometer. "I have a few spare minutes after my tea with Gizmo."

I could only hope that the lovely automaton had brewed an extra-large pot.

The engineer's interest in Gizmo may have started with a secret desire to discover her most delicious recipes, but it soon developed into a keen admiration for her mechanical mind. Since the train lingered long enough for the porter to deliver parcels, packages, and supplies, Mr. Jones always had time for a cup or two or three of Gizmo's tea.

"She awaits us at the Inn," Wally said. "But first, do you know which of your passengers is Professor Potts? I have a note to deliver."

"Dear me!" We all whirled to discover that the dapper dandy had contrived to creep up behind us.

"Apologies for eavesdropping. Couldn't be

helped!" He lifted his hat. "I'm Potts. Professor Potts."

I woofed softly. "Eavesdropping" is listening to the private conversations of others. It is *not* polite.

Potts glanced down at me, and in that unveiled instant I knew that not only was he no gentleman, he did not like dogs.

"Do I understand correctly?" His eyes lifted to Wally. "Your parents are absent? Terrible disappointment! I've wanted to get hold of the Kennewicketts for such a long time. Hard to catch them at symposiums." He glanced around. "Where the *devil* is Mr. Slade?"

I decided I did not like Professor Potts, either. He didn't smell buttery or delicious, and he had enormous feet.

"I'm Walter Kennewickett"—Wally shook Potts's hand—"and I'm afraid my parents' absence was unavoidable. Who is Mr. Slade?"

"New assistant." Professor Potts surveyed the crowd. "Just hired the fellow. Can't miss him. Marvelous mustache."

I dodged Professor Potts's feet as he turned about, apparently still searching for the unmissable Mr. Slade.

"He'll turn up," Mr. Jones said. "Unless he leaped from the train, he can't have left us."

When Potts stopped spinning, Wally handed him Calypso's note.

"Emergency, apparently," Professor Potts muttered as he read. "Couldn't be helped. Still, very disappointing. I've researched the Amazing Automated Inn. Electrons. Gyrating Generator. Automatons. Very impressive! Very impressive indeed. But I came for Oliver and Calypso, you see."

"I hope I can assist you in their

absence," Wally said. "Since Mr. Slade is missing, may I carry your bag, sir?"

"Kind of you." The professor nodded. "Very kind."

I followed Wally, Professor Potts, and Mr. Jones to the elevator.

We caught up with the vendors' convention in the lobby of the Inn. Mr. Jones scooped me up.

"Where's your wag, Noodles?" he asked, scratching my ears. "I've never seen you without it."

Where indeed? Still, I was thankful to be out from under the vendors' boots, even if I had to listen to Melvin telling the story of the Great Rescue. It was the reason a portrait of a pigeon hung in the Inn.

"On a bright, sunny morning, just like this one"—he always says that, even if it's foggy outside—"a rockslide took out the trestle over the Oblivion!"

"The raging river on the other side of Gasket Gully?" a popcorn vendor asked.

"The very same," Prissy assured him. "You just traveled over it by train."

Yawn.

"My father's pigeon Knitter Nap"—this is where he spins to point at the pigeon portrait—"flew to the next town, carrying a message that saved the train! Some of the Kennewicketts"—he looked meaningfully at Prissy, as if to say *The real Kennewicketts*—"have been raising heroic pigeons ever since."

Melvin's father had been no older than Melvin himself when he loosed the pigeon in the portrait, saving the train. He'd moved away a few years later, taking his birds and new bride with him.

"Melvin recently met with the mayor," Prissy said primly, "to let him know that, if needed, our pigeons will be ready!"

"Mail for Melvin," the porter, who had been sorting parcels in the corner, announced.

"Mail for me?" Melvin looked surprised. "I wasn't expecting anything." The porter handed him a blue box with stars and moons all over it.

The kind of box a mesmerizing magician might use in his act!

I barked a warning.

"Don't open that, Mel!" Wally shouted.

"Why ever not, nincompoop?" Melvin asked, pulling loose the twine that tied the box closed.

Wally jumped forward—

nd Professor Potts plunged into his path.

"Excuse me, sir!" Wally started to step past the professor.

"Certainly," Professor Potts cried as they both leaped left.

"Pardon!" the professor said as they both rotated right. "Apologies!" he sputtered. "Not intentional, I assure you!"

"If you would stand still, sir," Wally suggested politely, "I could make my way past."

"Of course!" Professor Potts assumed an academic pose, and Wally raced around him. But it was too late. Melvin had lifted the lid.

"Huzzah!" The popcorn vendors cheered as the contents hopped out. "A heroic pigeon!"

Wally sneezed.

The bird tipped its head sideways and fixed one eye on him. It fluffed its feathers. Wally sneezed again.

Prissy read the tag on the pigeon's leg. "'Iron Claw, pigeon extraordinaire. Property of Melvin Kennewickett'! Who could have sent it, Mel?"

"Doubtless a fan of my first-rate bird-racing skills," Melvin said. "I *am* well-known, Priss. The mayor came to see me! Pigeon extraordinaire, eh? Of course you are, Iron Claw!"

I shook my ears. What kind of name was that for a racing pigeon? The feathered faker didn't look the least bit extraordinaire to *me*. But he did look odd. He had one normal, beady eye, but the other was almost the size of a silver dime. It was black and white and patterned like a pinwheel.

"That's a bit peculiar," Mr. Jones said.

It was more than peculiar. It was unnatural.

The pigeon fluffed its feathers once more, and then *its pinwheel eye began to spin in a clockwise direction.*

"What an amazing eye!" Professor Potts exclaimed. "Just look at it!"

Melvin and Prissy leaned forward, and Iron Claw's eye spun faster.

"Now, that's *more* than a bit peculiar, don't you think, Walter?" Mr. Jones said, rubbing his chin. Wally did not reply. He was overcome with a fit of sneezing.

The eye, spinning at an incredible speed now, turned on Mr. Jones.

"I don't like the looks of that bird," the engineer declared.

The odd orb narrowed. If pigeons had brains, I would say that this one was not pleased with Mr. Jones.

"Nonsense!" Professor Potts countered. "I

believe this might be the most perfect pigeon in the world!"

"The most perfect pigeon in the world," Melvin repeated.

"You sound like a somniloquist, Melvin," Mr. Jones observed. "Have you been getting enough rest?"

A "somniloquist" is someone who talks in his sleep. The whole situation was growing more peculiar by the moment. Our guests stood, almost forgotten, watching the show as Gizmo studied Prissy and Melvin, her mechanical mind nearly clicking aloud.

"The most perfect pigeon in the world," repeated Prissy, sounding something like a somniloquist herself. "He will be our very special guest. Please bring a platter of pigeon food, Gizmo."

"A silver platter," Professor Potts suggested.

"I'll do nothing of the sort," Gizmo said. "Oliver and Calypso left me in charge of the Inn, and I say we will put that creature in the coop with its kin."

"No!" Professor Potts cried.

"Take him outside, Melvin," Gizmo instructed.

"I'm sorry, Gizmo," Melvin said. "I'm afraid I can't do that. He must stay with us."

"Nonsense," Gizmo said. "Calypso has been very clear about where birds belong. And we have guests to attend to!"

Iron Claw fluffed his feathers again, tipping his head and doubtless rattling his little bird brain. He spun his eye at Gizmo and blinked twice, but she did not relent. She marched across the room, took him from Melvin, and tossed him out the window.

"That's not fair," Melvin shouted, sounding completely himself again. "Iron Claw is *my* pet. You've never thrown Noodles out the window!"

"Of course she hasn't," Prissy pointed out. "That window is on the cliff side of the Inn. Dachshunds can't fly, after all."

I felt faint just thinking about it.

"No one is throwing Noodles out the window," Wally said, recovering from his sneezing fit.

"Never!" Mr. Jones growled. His arm tightened around me and he scratched my ears again.

"I must say," Professor Potts said, "pigeons appear to be the superior species. No diminutive *dachshund* could ever save a train. Am I right?"

I did *not* like Professor Potts.

"Is the entertainment over?" a popcorn vendor asked. Several started to cheer, as if they'd witnessed a magic show.

"Gentlemen," Gizmo said, clapping her hands, "if you will allow me to show you to your rooms? Professor Potts's lecture on the properties of perfectly popped corn will commence this evening followed by a demonstration of the Kennewicketts' new device."

"Walter," Mr. Jones whispered loudly as Gizmo whisked the crowd away, "would you and Noodles please join me in the locomotive?"

"But what about your tea, sir?" Wally asked. "And my invention?"

Mr. Jones looked grim. "I'm sorry, Walter. We must go at once. There is something I must show you."

10

I spent the long elevator ride clinging to the hope that whatever Mr. Jones intended to show us would banish my bat wings from Wally's mind. When we reached the cab of the locomotive, Mr. Jones pulled the *Washington Post* out from under a pile of papers.

"I knew that pigeon's peeper looked familiar," he said. "And I fear there is skullduggery afoot!" He handed the paper to Wally. There was a reproduction of a magician's handbill on the front page. A pigeon with a pinwheel eye was being held by a man in a cape. The fellow's face was mysteriously shadowed, but I could clearly see the curl of a mustache.

"'The Amazing Madini and His Peculiar Pigeon Disappear,'" Wally read aloud. "'Mr.

Madini, whose pigeon peered into the eyes of audience members while Madini mesmerized them with his

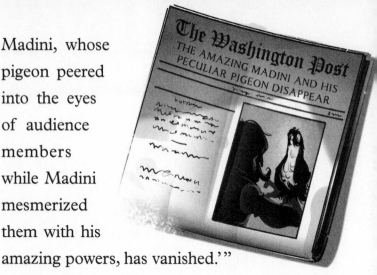

amazing powers, has vanished.'"

Mesmerized?! The last shred of fear that I would have to demonstrate the vest today fled me. The game was afoot, as Mr. Arthur Conan Doyle's dauntless detective Sherlock Holmes would say. I was saved.

"This could explain my cousins' curious behavior," Wally said, looking up. "But you weren't affected, Mr. Jones."

"I have a natural immunity to the hypnotic arts," Mr. Jones explained. Apparently, dachshunds do as well. But then, we have a surprising number of superior traits. "You will notice that Gizmo was not affected either. And you were sneezing too hard for the hypnotism to take effect. Keep reading, Walter."

"'Authorities are seeking Madini,'" Wally read on, "'for questioning in the puzzling case of Mrs. Birdy Pringle, banking heiress, who has been cooing at her financier husband for a week. The heiress, who now refuses to eat anything but bread crumbs, has tried multiple times to leap from the window of their mansion, thinking she could fly.'"

Just like the pasha! This, then, was the fate of those who fell completely under the Mesmers' control.

"'The sad socialite was publicly mesmerized by the magician three times the week before he and his pigeon flew the coop. She appeared to be the ideal subject.'" He lowered the paper. "The bird in the picture must be Iron Claw!"

"So the magician shipped his pigeon to the Automated Inn," Mr. Jones said. "But why? And where is Madini himself?"

Where indeed? I wondered if Wally was

thinking of the mysterious Mr. Slade, whose own vanishing act had caused Professor Potts such consternation. Mr. Jones checked his chronometer, tapped the pressure gauge. "Time is short, Walter. What can be done?"

"Will you send a wire from the station at your next stop, Mr. Jones?" Wally asked. He was using his amazing brain to analyze the situation and devise a suitable solution. Our station had no telegraph, but Mr. Jones's next stop did.

"A wire?" Mr. Jones asked.

"To Edith Roosevelt," Wally explained. "At the White House. It should read, 'Franz has come calling.'"

I knew instantly that this was a clever reference to Franz Mesmer. Mrs. Roosevelt would know instantly too.

"'. . . Holding the fort. Hope to see TR and friends at their soonest convenience. Walter Ke—' *Ah-choo!*"

"Bless you!" Mr. Jones gave Wally a handkerchief.

"I meant Kennewickett, of course," Wally

said, wiping his nose. "Walter K. Kennewickett."

"That's incredibly cryptic, Walter." Mr. Jones nodded. "It has something to do with the missing magic act as well as where your parents are, I'll wager."

I whined. If something is "cryptic" it has a hidden meaning. Mr. Jones was too clever not to catch such a clue.

"And I have never had cause to contact the White House before," the engineer added.

"I wish I could explain, sir." Wally flushed. "But I have promises to keep."

Wally is smart *and* dependable.

"And the train must run on time," Mr. Jones said, consulting his pocket chronometer. "I am loath to leave you like this, Walter."

"There may be danger," Wally admitted. "But the most helpful thing you can do is get a message to Mrs. Roosevelt!"

"I see," mused Mr. Jones. "You've fallen headfirst into some confounding conspiracy and are not at liberty to reveal it, even to me."

I stood transfixed. Could it be? I could almost

hear Oliver's voice. *The fact that Mr. Jones has never once been right doesn't mean he never will be.* Had it happened at last? Had the amazing engineer unraveled the Mesmer mystery, menacing magicians and all?

"I have it figured." Mr. Jones winked. "Never fear."

Wally flushed even redder.

"I'll send your message, Walter, and be back the day after tomorrow. In the meantime, beware that brilliant bird!"

"The brilliant *bird?*" Wally blinked. "You think a clever Columbidae could be the mastermind behind the Mesmer . . . er, this mesmerizing magic act?"

I sat down. Calypso was correct after all. Mr. Jones certainly would make an extraordinary writer of fiction.

"I have long felt that there was something sinister about pigeons." Mr. Jones lowered his voice. "Haven't you noticed? They're everywhere. Watching. Listening. So the feathered fiends are finally making their move, eh? Be careful, Walter. Don't let the wrong pigeon in!"

"I will be careful, sir," Wally said, folding the paper and putting it in his pocket. "Gizmo will not let *any* pigeons into the Inn. Mother would *not* approve."

"I'm sure you are right," Mr. Jones commented as we climbed out of the cab. "I am confident that the amazing Gizmo is up to the challenge."

"Yes, sir," Wally agreed.

"One more thing!" Mr. Jones said, leaning out the window. "Your cousins appeared to fall under the pigeon's power the moment his eye began to spin. They recovered quickly, but be careful, Walter. I don't want to find any of you pecking at bread crumbs on the lawn when I return."

Wally picked me up, and we watched until the locomotive was lost in the billows of steam from its stack.

"Mr. Jones was *almost* right, Noodles." Wally

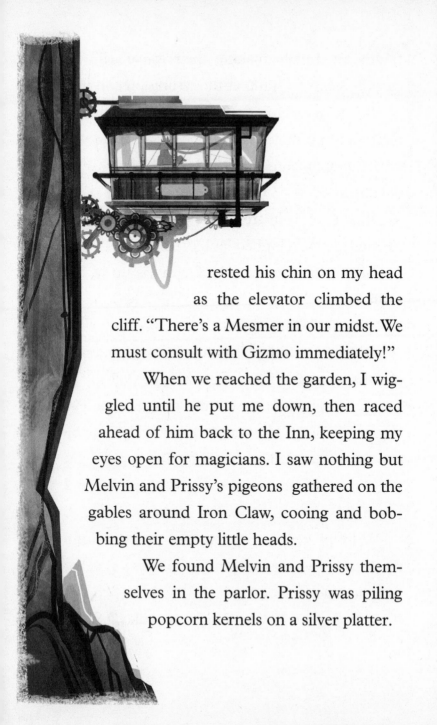

rested his chin on my head as the elevator climbed the cliff. "There's a Mesmer in our midst. We must consult with Gizmo immediately!"

When we reached the garden, I wiggled until he put me down, then raced ahead of him back to the Inn, keeping my eyes open for magicians. I saw nothing but Melvin and Prissy's pigeons gathered on the gables around Iron Claw, cooing and bobbing their empty little heads.

We found Melvin and Prissy themselves in the parlor. Prissy was piling popcorn kernels on a silver platter.

"What are you doing, Priss?" Wally asked.

"Pigeons love popcorn," Prissy said sweetly. "I want to see Iron Claw again. Come with me, Walter."

"Priss!" Wally said. "You should leave that bird alone. It has muddled your mind!"

Wally was right. She was actually being nice.

"Mr. Slade said he'd like you to take a good look at Iron Claw," Melvin said, reaching for Walter.

"Mr. Slade?" Wally asked, backing away.

"Yes. He purports to be a humble assistant," Melvin replied, as Wally dodged his grasp again. Wally has become very good at avoiding Melvin in the past few months.

"'Purports'?" Wally asked from a safe distance.

"I feel sure he is more than he appears," Melvin said. "He is quite knowledgeable about Columbidae, eh, Priss?"

"He agrees that Iron Claw is exceptional," Prissy concurred. "You *insisted* on sneezing,

Walter, so you couldn't see it. But one peep at that praiseworthy pigeon and I'm sure you will agree. How I wish he were mine!"

"But he's not." Melvin smiled smugly. He gave up on collaring Wally and opened the door for Priss instead. "Let's go admire him!"

"Wait!" Wally called after them as they went out. "Does Mr. Slade have a mustache, by any chance?"

I wagged. Walter Kennewickett had noticed the mustache, too!

"A magnificent mustache!" Melvin called back. "It curls."

11

We found Gizmo in the kitchen, oiling the household staff. Suds, the scullery maid, was always in danger of developing squeaks. The footmen were less susceptible, but Gizmo inspected them diligently just the same.

Everyone smiled or nodded as we came in. I had never met an automaton that did not like Walter Kennewickett. Even Jeeves had had a soft spot for him, before he lost his head.

"Mr. Jones suspects there is skullduggery afoot," Wally said, holding up the paper.

Gizmo scanned the headline. "I concur." She set down the oilcan and took the paper from Wally's hand. "I've developed a keen admiration for that engineer."

"We all have," Talos, the footman, agreed.

"Aside from his occasional odd idea, he is an extraordinary man."

The assistant cook, Knives, snicked agreement from the corner. Knives communicates entirely by means of bladed attachments. His snicks, clicks, and occasional *shhiiink* can actually be quite eloquent, even while using a shears attachment on one hand and a cleaver on the other to trim and chop stew meat for dinner.

Gizmo glanced up from her reading. "I don't suppose Jones mentioned the secret ingredient in his snickerdoodles?"

"I'm afraid the subject didn't come up," Wally said as I snapped up a little something Knives tossed to me, comforted in knowing that if I barked an alarm, an army of automatons with sharp wits and sharper attachments would deal with any dastards who attempted to mesmerize my Wally.

Gizmo handed the paper back. "It appears there was no need for your parents to leave, Walter. The Mesmers were making their way to us! Do you think it's the Automated Inn they are after?"

"I feel it's more likely they have their eye on the Very Important People who come here," Wally said. "I sent TR a message, requesting that my parents return."

"Well done, Walter! A telegram sent by Mr. Jones at his next stop, I assume?"

Wally nodded. "He suspects that the pigeon Iron Claw is the mastermind of a clever conspiracy."

"Of course he does." Gizmo sighed. "Talos *did* mention his occasional odd ideas. I'm prone to think this Mesmer uses his pigeon's peculiar eye to capture the audience's attention, allowing him to mesmerize them more easily. We must find this meddlesome magician and detain him until your parents arrive. I suspect Professor Potts."

"I would agree if I had not just met Melvin in the parlor," Wally said slowly. "He spoke of a mustachioed *Mr. Slade* who'd like me to take a good look at Iron Claw. And you can see from the photo that Madini has an impressive mustache as well."

Gizmo tapped the newspaper. "But this *could* be Potts with a mustache. The man was certainly meddlesome when you attempted to prevent Melvin from opening the box."

That was putting it mildly. The man had been a menace.

"Perhaps," Wally said uncertainly. "But Professor Potts might just as easily be a victim of the Mesmers, forced to follow their foul commands!"

Gizmo's finely geared brain whirred as she considered.

"I agree," she said at last. "The mastermind may be cunningly concealed and using Potts as a decoy, or we could have multiple Mesmers on the grounds." She sighed. "I suppose we can't simply lock all of Calypso's guests in their rooms willy-nilly. We must watch and wait until they make a move. It's fortunate you are allergic to feathers, Walter. You escaped the pigeon's effect."

"But Melvin and Prissy are not so lucky," Wally pointed out. "They've already exhibited signs of falling under the Mesmers' power. Perhaps you could lock *them* up?"

"It would be logical," Gizmo agreed. "But after the unfortunate incident with Jeeves, automatons are not allowed to detain or deter Kennewickett family members. Our wiring would ignite if we so much as attempted it. We are going to have to leave them to their own devices until your parents return. Focus on your own safety, Walter. Allergies might not protect you again."

"Agreed," Talos said, tossing Suds a towel as she headed to the sink. "You are still at risk, Walter."

"An anti-mesmerism device might be attempted," Wally suggested.

"Excellent," Gizmo approved. "Focus on your experiments, and leave the rest to us." She clapped her hands, and the staff came to attention. "As you've heard, we have at least one miscreant among us. Be alert. Be aware." She pulled a Dust Bunny out of her pocket, wound it, and set it on the floor. "Be everywhere! These Mesmers must learn they are messing with the wrong inn!"

The automatons clicked, snicked, hummed, and shouted agreement. It was a very encouraging cacophony.

"Knives," Gizmo continued when they had quieted, "I believe Walter needs a bodyguard."

Knives nodded and attached his most intimidating instruments of cutlery before following us down to the lab. He stationed himself strategically outside the door. I must admit I was glad for the backup.

I watched while Wally gathered tools and supplies from his parents' work stations, then set about magnifying the newspaper's illustration of Iron Claw's unsettling eye. He took precise measurements, made meticulous calculations, then fed the particulars into Calypso's Analytical Engines and attached the drafting mechanism. Multiple mechanical hands in white cotton gloves dipped pens in inkwells and began to draw a larger-than-life-size copy of the awful orb. Meanwhile, Wally worked on a contraption to make the image spin.

When he was done, he took the cleverly

drawn copy and fixed it to his rotator, set the mechanical hands of the Analytical Engines to shake him soundly in ten seconds, then stood before the rotator and turned it on. Wally was clearly not immune to the hypnotic arts. He wobbled, then swayed, but multiple hands gloved in white cotton caught him and shook him from his mesmerized state.

"Excellent!" he exclaimed, sorting through lenses he'd collected from Oliver's side of the lab. He fitted one after another into his goggles, standing before the horrible eye each time he made an adjustment.

Gizmo brought plates down for dinner.

We ate quickly and Wally went back to work.

I went to my pillow. A well-rested dachshund is a well-prepared dachshund, after all!

I watched as long as dachshundly possible before I closed my eyes.

I was dreaming of sausage links when Wally shook me awake.

"I've done it, Noodles," he said. "I've completely countered the hypnotic effect. What do you think?"

The motorized monocle on Wally's right eye spun spirals in a counterclockwise direction. His magnificent left eye was magnified behind multiple layers of lenses. I thought that, considering how hard he had been working, it was perfectly natural that his hair was standing on end.

I licked his nose.

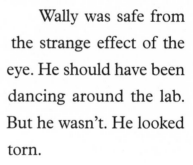

Wally was safe from the strange effect of the eye. He should have been dancing around the lab. But he wasn't. He looked torn.

"What of Melvin and Prissy, Noodles?" he asked. "If they fall completely under the Mesmers' control, it will be the end of them." A strange and dark expression flickered across Wally's face. "The end of their cruel games. There would be no one to ridicule my allergies. No further feathers in my bed." His voice grew as terrible as his expression. "No one would ever call me *nincompoop* or *runt* again!"

Walter Kennewickett whirled . . . and caught sight of his own reflection in Calypso's mirror.

He crossed the lab and stood staring into his own eyes. His hand went to his heart, and I knew what he was pondering. *Which sort of Kennewickett am I going to be?*

I held my breath, knowing that this is precisely the kind of moment when the question of whether a Kennewickett is generally good or abominably bad is decided. Not when the world is watching, but when they are almost alone. When they could walk away and no one but their loyal dachshund would know that they could have tried . . . but didn't.

A vision of the pasha who had flung himself from the clock tower flashed through my mind, and strangely, he had Melvin's face.

"No," Wally whispered. "I will help them. I must!"

I shivered with relief. Wally was himself once more.

He wasted no time constructing a pair of goggles identical to his own for Melvin, then turned to Calypso's collection of millinery.

"Now comes the difficult part, Noodles— preparing a pair for Prissy."

I felt *impossible part* might be a more precise phrase. Prissy turns up her nose at Calypso's finest hats; she is not likely to wear a mechanical mess, no matter how useful, on her face. Still, Wally tried. He selected an assortment of materials, including lengths of pink ribbon and a purple faux feather before he sat down at his bench.

"Finished," Wally said at last, holding up his creation. "What do you think?"

Even if my tail had not been malfunctioning, I could not have wagged encouragement.

"I know," Wally said sadly. "But I've done my best. Come on!" He straightened his shoulders and marched out of the lab. Knives and I followed him up the stairs.

We found Melvin and Prissy standing in the back of the dining hall, listening to Professor Potts's lecture on the correct color of corn. Gizmo was close at hand, clearly watching over them. Wally wisely held the extra sets of headgear he'd created behind his back as we approached, even though he was wearing his own.

"What nincompoopery is this, runt?" Melvin asked when he saw Wally's coat and goggles.

"Your minds are in danger," Wally whispered. "There are . . ." I could see him struggling over whether to reveal the truth. But sometimes promises must be broken. ". . . mesmerizing magicians among us. He . . . or they . . . are using Iron Claw's odd eye to gain control of your minds!"

Melvin laughed.

"Have you gone mad, Walter?" Prissy asked. "That's what comes of hanging around with hobos, I suppose."

"Priss," Wally said. "You must listen to me. The hobo was President Theodore Roosevelt. He came here to request our help in defeating this very foe. You are in danger! Ask Gizmo."

"Ask the automaton that threw my present out the window?" Melvin looked incredulously at the automaton in question.

"I am wired for honesty," Gizmo assured him. "Walter is telling you the truth."

"Will you at least try them on," Wally urged, "and keep them with you?"

"Of *course* we won't," Prissy whispered. "We'd look ridiculous, Walter."

"*Please,* Priss?" Wally's hugely magnified eye was magnificently earnest.

"No. And don't stand beside us. The popcorn vendors might think we are related."

"We *are* related," Wally whispered back as a vendor turned to look.

"Yes, but they don't have to know that," said Prissy. "Go away!"

Most of the vendors were looking at Wally now. I felt that he was strikingly handsome in his lab coat and headgear, but he self-consciously shoved the extra goggles in his pocket and took a step back. Professor Potts had stopped speaking. Everyone was staring at Wally now.

"Do something, Mel," Prissy pleaded.

"Please ignore our little friend," Melvin announced, making circles in the air with his index finger as if to indicate a sadly addled mind. "We must not encourage his delusions."

"Melvin!" Gizmo said. "Walter is not delusional!"

"Of course the machines here are *mad* about him." Melvin executed his annoying finger circle once more. "Their brains are full of metal things going round and round as well. Am I right?" He laughed, and the vendors laughed with him. Some of them even pointed at Wally and held their sides.

A man I had not seen before stepped into the room. A man with a massive mustache, and strange black eyes. He was carrying a sheaf of papers. *Could this be the elusive Mr. Slade?*

"Is that some sort of invention on the boy's face, Melvin?" he asked.

"Invention?" Melvin laughed. "Wally does not *invent,* Mr. Slade."

It was *Mr. Slade!* But was he the Mesmer in our midst? The man was certainly singular, but Professor Potts still had my vote.

"At least not things that actually work," Prissy was saying. "Those are . . . spectacles. The poor child is terribly nearsighted."

"Priss!" Gizmo exclaimed, but Mr. Slade ignored the automaton and marched to the front of the hall.

"The notes you requested from your room, sir!" He bowed as he handed the papers to Professor Potts.

"It took you long enough, Slade," Potts snapped, then looked pointedly at Wally. "If you are quite done disturbing my lecture, I'd like to go on."

Gizmo put her hand on Wally's shoulder and drew him toward the door.

"You've done your best," she said. "They don't appear to be in imminent danger. Knives can stay here and watch over them. Would you mind fetching the bolts from the basement, Walter? It is time for the demonstration of your mother's device!"

Wally's shoulders sagged as we trudged back to the dungeons. To have overcome so many difficulties of function and design only to be defeated by ignorance and jest would have been hard for a scientist six times his age.

I waited while Wally transferred several lightning bolts into bottles, then followed him upstairs.

Our timing was excellent. Professor Potts had just finished his lecture, and the vendors had gathered in the great room for the demonstration. They chuckled, still amused by Wally's eyewear, as he placed a bottle in the popper.

"Now, Walter," Gizmo instructed. Wally pulled the lever, and lightning laced through the machine. The kernels of popcorn inside exploded into a snowdrift of scrumptiousness. The salesmen gasped, then cheered.

"More! More! More!" Mr. Slade called.

"Yes, yes, more!" all the popcorn vendors echoed. We must try it for ourselves!" Their former mirth at Wally's odd appearance was seemingly forgotten in the excitement of the moment.

Wally spent the rest of the evening happily running up and down the stairs, his arms full of bottled bolts, his magnified eye on the lookout for Mesmers. Keeping up with him was exhausting.

By the time everyone had tried the machine, Melvin and Prissy had slipped away. The vendors headed to their beds without a single sinister happening.

Wally and I went to the lab for one last look at Oliver's experimental data.

"Less than a sizzle left," he observed as we passed the Voltage Vats. "The Popper was

certainly popular, Noodles. We'll have to collect more electrons for Mother after Father's
experiment is done."

He noted the reading on every atmosphere-
related gauge, gadget, and device, then yawned.

"Walter," Gizmo said from the doorway.
"Get some sleep. We automatons will watch over
the Inn tonight."

"Thank you, Gizmo." Wally sighed. "I fear
I'm missing something important, but . . . I can
do no more."

We retired to his room, where he hung his
new eyewear beside his lab coat on the back of
the door. Even after he fell asleep, he tossed and
turned and mumbled about Mesmers.

Poor Wally. I licked his ear until the night-
mares went away.

12

The next morning I shivered awake, trying to shake free from a terrible dream. I had been flying through fluffy clouds. Baby angels with white feathered wings kept calling me "Pidge" and trying to feed me popcorn kernels from a silver platter. The events of the previous day had made me forget the horrible vest and frightening wings, but somehow they had crept into my dreams.

I crawled out of the covers and sniffed, sensing something was amiss. The room was dark, but I could discern no danger lurking in the corners.

I walked to the end of the bed and tipped my head one way and then the other. Giving the head a little tip often shakes loose an idea or two.

The wind howled outside the window, and thunder rumbled in the distance . . . The expected electrical storm was close at hand. Suddenly, I realized what was missing.

Bacon. I didn't smell bacon. Or sausage or pancakes or eggs or toast.

We had an inn full of guests, and *Gizmo was not cooking breakfast!* Something was terribly wrong.

I barked an alarm.

Wally slipped his lab coat on over his pajamas and pulled on his goggles before we hurried into the hall. There were Dust Bunnies everywhere. But they were not capering, cavorting, or cleaning. They weren't moving at all—because they hadn't been wound!

"Gizmo!" Wally cried. We raced down the stairs.

Gizmo was motionless in her closet.

"It's her electric cells," Wally said, checking the gauge. "They're almost empty!"

"I suspect sabotage," Gizmo whispered when

Wally leaned close. "The Me . . . *z* . . . *z* . . . *z* . . . *zzz-zzzt!*" And she went still.

"Sabotage" is the deliberate destruction of important equipment.

Such as—

"The Gyrating Generator!" Wally exclaimed. This time we raced for the roof. The wind was whipping around the Inn, so the generator should have been whirling wildly, producing plenty of power. But it wasn't.

I fought my fear while Wally fought his way up the ladder, buffeted by the blustery breeze. It took him less than two minutes to reappear. He slid down the ladder like a fireman and scooped me up.

"Pigeon nests," Wally said, and sneezed three times. "Twigs, sticks, and feathers in all the moving parts! It shouldn't affect Father's lightning collection. I'll need to wear a mask to clean it out once the danger of lightning has passed. Perhaps Mr. Jones can help."

Waiting for Mr. Jones seemed like an excellent

idea to me. He was due at the station within the hour, and his train always arrived on schedule.

"In the meantime, let's find Knives. He may still have power. We need backup, Noodles!"

But when we reached the kitchen, a chill went down my spine. All of the automatons were still, but Knives was not just frozen in place. He was frozen in several places at once. *Someone had taken off his arms.* His wicked-looking bladed attachments were lying silent and useless on opposite sides of the room.

Wally ran his hand through his hair. "We need the automatons. And the automatons need power. To the lab, Noodles!"

We raced downstairs to the dungeons and flung open the laboratory door. Wally looked in dismay at the small sizzle of electrons that remained in the vat.

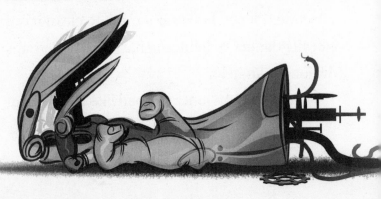

"Emptying the Voltage Vats must have been part of their plan," he said. "The Mesmers are more dangerous than we imagined."

Wally studied Oliver's instruments. He bit his lip.

"I'm sorry, Father," he said, then pulled the lever that would send the electrons from the Lightning Collectors not to Oliver's transmitter, but into the Voltage Vats. Next, he checked the wiring on the Vats themselves. The old system was still in place. I had never been so proud of Wally. He was thinking clearly and acting decisively in the face of disaster. If his plan worked, the first bolt of lightning striking the Atmospheric Electron Collectors on the rooftop would completely recharge the Inn. Gizmo would come instantly to life, muster the staff, and defeat the Mesmers.

"We have guests, Noodles," Wally said grimly when he was done. "We must do our best to take care of them."

I followed my hero up the stairs to confront the waiting Mesmers.

When we reached the lobby, we found the popcorn vendors sitting on the floor in their pajamas, slippers, and robes eating bowls of stale popcorn. Melvin and Prissy were perched on the reception desk. Professor Potts's assistant, Mr. Slade, stood above them, Iron Claw atop his head.

"I don't like the look of this, Noodles," Wally whispered. I was certain Gizmo did not like it either, though all she could do was stare helplessly from her open closet.

"We've been waiting for you, Walter," Mr. Slade said.

"May I assume I am addressing the magician Madini?" Wally asked.

"In person," Mr. Slade—er, Madini replied.

"What have you done with Professor Potts?" Wally asked.

"We disposed of him," Madini said, looking at the window.

I gasped. I had not liked Professor Potts, but no one deserved *that*.

"And . . . and what are your plans for our inn?" Wally asked.

You may think that was uncaring. But I had noticed that evil geniuses in books delight in discussing their dastardly plans. Clearly, Wally had noted this weakness as well. He was "buying time," as the saying goes.

"The Inn? We have no plans for the Inn," Madini mocked. "It's the president we are pursuing. Oh, yes! We knew of his ingenious disguise as well as his destination."

"You knew Mr. Roosevelt was coming here! But how?"

"We have our ways. Our only mistake was taking the train. Roosevelt arranged his own transportation and arrived before we did. So thank you for sending such an urgent plea for his return, Walter. We feared he had escaped!"

13

Madini rubbed his hands together. "Our spies inform us that due to your dispatch, the president's coach is rushing to your aid even as we speak. And as soon as he opens that door, he will be ours!"

"Melvin! Prissy!" Walter shouted. "Wake up! Our president is in peril!" Prissy made a strange cooing sound, and Melvin flapped his elbows.

"They currently believe they are Columbidae, I'm afraid," Madini said, and twirled the tips of his mustache. "But we have plans for you, too, young Kennewickett! You will help us capture the president!"

"Why do you keep saying *we* and *us*?" Wally asked.

"You dare to question us?" Madini thundered. "Silence!"

"I don't think these popcorn vendors are on your side at all," Wally went on. "I think you have mesmerized them. I believe you are attempting to imply that you have allies, when in reality you are all alone."

"You believe your ridiculous eyewear will protect you!" Madini laughed. "Let's put your invention to the test!" Thunder growled outside the window. Iron Claw bobbed his feathered head. His pinwheel eye began to spin.

"Pigeons are perfect," the confused crowd said.

"Pigeons are per-*choo!*" Wally took a handkerchief from his pocket. "I meant perfect, of course."

"We don't believe you," Madini said, bobbing his head like a bird.

Wally is not a very good actor. But he is almost as good as a dachshund at the art of detection.

"Mind transference!" Wally declared, dropping the attempted deception. His magnified eye focused on Iron Claw. The pigeon stared back at him, pinwheel spinning, and for one moment their eyes locked. "Madini is somehow sharing Iron Claw's mind, Noodles!"

I had never heard a pigeon laugh before. It is a horrible, horrible sound.

"And Iron Claw was lurking outside the window of the locomotive when I relayed my message!" Wally went on. "That's why I sneezed!"

"Correct!" Iron Claw said in Madini's voice. It was more terrible than anything ever written by Mr. Edgar Allan Poe. "And now you *must* join us, young Kennewickett. No one can know our secret and go free!"

"Mr. Jones's theory was more accurate than we thought," Wally marveled. "He is an extremely smart man!"

At that moment, there was a rumble of strange thunder, and the shutters of the Inn shook.

"We won't have to worry about Jones much longer," Madini and Iron Claw said in unison. "We are not all alone, you see. We have comrades in this cause."

"Walter's unusual eyewear is protecting him from our power," Iron Claw cooed. "Take it from him, my minions."

The popcorn vendors rose as one.

I leaped in front of Wally, ready to attack any ankle that dared to come near.

"Melvin, Prissy," Madini commanded. "Toss that disruptive dachshund out the window. And once he's out, why not take a nice flight yourselves? Flap away, little birds!" Melvin and Prissy hopped down from the desk and started toward me.

Thinking quickly, I knocked over a bowl of buttery popcorn. Puffed kernels scattered across the floor. Melvin and Prissy were after them in an instant, pecking like the pigeons they believed themselves to be.

"Brilliant, Noodles!" Wally cried.

"Attack, my minions!" Iron Claw ordered, spreading his wings. The popcorn vendors lurched toward us. *"Get those goggles!"* Several moments of mayhem ensued.

I dodged between trampling feet, snatching slippers when I could to slow the vendors down. Wally ducked under outstretched arms and eluded frantic fingers. Melvin and Prissy hopped about, unwittingly disrupting the popcorn vendors' attempts to capture Wally.

And then three things happened at almost the same instant: Wally's hair stood on end, indicating that lightning had struck the Electron Collectors. Gizmo, suddenly sizzling with electricity, stepped out of her closet. And the front door flew open, revealing Theodore Roosevelt, Oliver, and Calypso.

"It's a trap, Mr. President!" Wally cried, grabbing up a loose bedroom slipper and flinging it at Iron Claw.

The pigeon was forced to duck, giving Wally time to call out, "Cover your eyes, sir! The pigeon shares the Mesmer's mind! He manipulates people by means of his unnatural eye!"

"I assume your unusual headgear offers protection?" Oliver called over the crowd.

"It does, Father," Wally agreed.

"And did you create additional devices?" Calypso queried.

"I did, Mother." Wally pulled the goggles he'd made for Melvin and Prissy from his lab coat pocket and hurled them over the heads of the milling minions.

Iron Claw lifted off of Madini's head, attempting to grab the goggles from the air. Oliver leaped, stretching to snag them before the pigeon could snatch them away.

If I hadn't paused to see who would reach the goggles first, Melvin never would have caught me. He tucked me under his wing and hopped wildly for the window.

Prissy had already pushed it open, revealing the stormy sky above and sheer cliff below. I confess, I cried out.

Melvin had almost made it to the window when Wally caught his coattail. Melvin turned to peck at Wally's hand, and I wiggled free.

Iron Claw had returned to Madini's head. His pinwheel eye was spinning wildly. *"Get Roosevelt,"* he cooed.

"Get Roosevelt!" Madini screamed.

"Roo-se-velt, Roo-se-velt," the mob of mesmerized merchants murmured, making for the president.

But they hadn't counted on the courageous Kennewicketts.

Oliver and Calypso stood shoulder to shoulder in front of the commander in chief, their protective headgear in place.

TR had clearly been coaching them in the oriental art of hand-to-hand combat. I couldn't help but feel some amount of pride in their obvious skill. Popcorn vendors fell before them one after another, tossed, turned, and shaken.

Wally leaped onto the desk to confront Iron Claw and Madini. "Surrender!" he cried, assuming a most effective judo stance. "Your minions are use—*ah-choo!*" He pulled the handkerchief from his pocket. "I meant useless, of course!"

Madini pulled something from *his* pocket and threw it to the floor. There was a fantastic flash and the furious flapping of wings.

When the smoke cleared, Madini and Iron Claw were gone.

"Curses!" Oliver cried. "They have escaped!"

"Quite," Calypso agreed, pulling off her goggles. "Fled to fight another day." She surveyed the room. "Hair, Walter! Melvin, Prissy, *stop that irritating hopping this instant, and the rest of you sit down!*"

Melvin and Prissy stopped hopping, and the vendors sat. Prissy put her hand to her head. Melvin's eyes widened when he saw Theodore Roosevelt.

"Mr. President?" he said. Calypso appeared to have cured them of their mesmerized state. This was hardly a surprise to me. We had once been visited by a tyrant who was reluctant to try Gizmo's blue-ribbon meatloaf. Calypso had commanded him to cease complaining and eat, and the despotic diplomat had polished off his entire plate and asked most humbly for more.

Prissy, apparently realizing she had been hopping about in her nightclothes, burst into tears.

"Now, now, all's well that ends well, dearest," Calypso said, hugging her as the household staff rushed belatedly to the rescue. Knives had even collected his cutlery after someone had apparently reattached his arms.

Calypso released Prissy and clapped her hands. "We have guests to attend to, everyone."

Theodore Roosevelt examined Oliver's goggles while Calypso, Oliver, Gizmo, Melvin, and Prissy set the popcorn vendors to rights. The staff focused on fixing the furniture.

"I ruined your experiment, Father," confessed Wally. "And broke your confidence by telling your secret, Mr. President. I'm sorry, Mother." Wally removed his protective eyewear, and suddenly he looked very small. "I've allowed Professor Potts to be thrown out the window."

Melvin walked to the window in question, flung it open, and leaned out into the storm.

"He's still there," Melvin announced.

"What!" TR cried. "Is it possible?"

"Potts is clinging to a ledge by his fingertips as I speak, sir," Melvin assured him.

A rescue was instantly organized and expertly executed by the president himself. When the professor had been pulled safely inside, TR turned to Wally. "Buck up, Walter," he said. "We've won the day, thanks to you."

At that precise and celebratory moment, the mayor of Gasket Gully stepped through the still-open door.

14

We must prepare a pigeon, Melvin!" the mayor yelled over the rumble of thunder. "We need a Kennewickett bird to carry a message to the train! An explosion has destroyed the trestle."

Wally looked at me. The strange rumble we'd heard hadn't been thunder. It had been Madini's "comrades" *blowing the trestle to bits!*

"Huzzah!" the popcorn vendors shouted, clearly not fully recovered from their mesmerized melee. "A heroic pigeon!"

Calypso quickly penned a note to Mr. Jones, and we rushed to the coop.

It was empty. Iron Claw and Madini had taken every last pigeon with them when they fled.

"The villain!" Melvin cried. "How could I ever have admired him?"

"This is disappointing," the mayor declared. "We've always felt the Kennewicketts could be counted on in an emergency."

"No one could have prepared for this," President Roosevelt said sadly. "Not even this brave family."

"Ahem." Wally pulled the winged vest from his lab coat pocket. "Noodles can carry the message."

"Noodles?" The mayor blinked as if he had misunderstood. "You mean your *dachshund,* Walter? Surely his little legs are not sufficient for such an endeavor!"

Everyone looked around. They didn't see me, of course. Dachshunds are very good at disappearing.

"Noodles!" Wally called. I looked at the tail tucked between my legs, and suddenly, I knew. Kennewicketts aren't the only ones who must face the terrible testing of their hearts and wills.

The conundrum comes to dachshunds as well. I knew I could never be as brave or resourceful as Walter Kennewickett. But what sort of dachshund was I? The kind who hid when he heard his best friend call? Never! I forced my legs to move.

"There you are, Noodles," Wally said as I crept out from under the foliage. And before anyone could say, "Dachshunds can't fly," he was strapping the wings on me.

The endless sky stretched dark and stormy above me, as if it would pull me away from Wally forever.

"Walter!" the president exclaimed, leaning over us. "Is this Attempt One Thousand and One to achieve powered controlled flight?"

"It's no attempt, sir," Wally said, fastening the last button. "I would never have managed it if not for your inspirational words!"

"Bully!" the president cheered. "Who needs a heroic pigeon when you have a daring dachshund?"

Wally patted my head. "Dachshunds aren't daring, sir. But they are dependable!"

"Dependability will have to suffice," Oliver said.

The train whistle sounded in the distance.

"It's life or death, Noodles." Wally gave me the note. "You must get this message to Mr. Jones!"

"If that amazing man dies, the secret of his snickerdoodles dies with him," Gizmo cried, pressing her hand to her bosom. "Save him for me, Noodles!"

I closed my eyes and willed my wagger to wiggle. Nothing happened. *Tail failure may cause tragedy.*

Wally squatted down. "You can do it, boy," he whispered.

I shook the fear out of my ears and focused on Wally's voice.

"You can do it, Noodles!" Wally said so loudly everyone heard.

I licked his nose, and then ran in a circle. My wings flapped once. The wagger was working.

"*You can do it, Noodles!*" Wally shouted again.

I raced across the yard, wagging with all my might. The president cheered as I lifted off . . . and then I was falling up into the terrifying sky. Only . . . I wasn't falling. Not at all! Walter Kennewickett had achieved powered and *controlled* flight. All I had to do was point my nose. I looped the loop and saw the surprised look on Prissy's face as I circled. I saw Melvin's mouth fall open. I saw the mayor faint. He needed someone to lick his ears, but I had no time for that now—I had to fly!

I pointed my nose into the storm and wagged for all I was worth. I saw the locomotive coming. It was rounding the last bend before the Oblivion River Gully!

I had to wag faster . . .

Faster, faster, faster . . .

. . . Too fast! The locomotive steamed past me, and the wind it generated tumbled me onto the muddy ground.

The train slowed as it started up the incline, but I knew I couldn't catch it. The mayor was right—my legs were too short. It was the end for Mr. Jones and his amazing snickerdoodles.

You can do it.

I rubbed the mud from my muzzle. Dachshunds have a very good grasp of the general principles of science. I knew sound could not travel all the way from the Inn. I wasn't hearing Wally's voice with my ears. I was hearing it in my heart.

You can do it, Noodles. Dachshunds aren't daring, but they are dependable.

I jumped up on the iron track and started to run.

Dependable, snickerdoodle, Wally, Wally, Wally, the train's wheels hummed on the rails. I ran faster.

Wally, Wally, Wally, they sang right in front of my nose. *Wally!* My wag was back. I was airborne!

Caboose . . . cars . . . people pointing . . .

Locomotive!

I locked my wings and dived.

Mr. Jones was astonished when I flew through the window. But he thought fast when I dropped the message into his hand.

"Hit the brakes," he bellowed. "The trestle is out!"

EPILOGUE

And that is how the Great Mesmer War began.

Mr. Jones stopped the train, of course, and though it was late for the first time since the first Great Rescue, the passengers were saved. He was so pleased at being correct about Iron Claw that he shared his secret snickerdoodle recipe with Gizmo.

Melvin and Prissy actually told Wally that they were sorry and suggested that he might just be a real Kennewickett after all. Oliver noted their apology in his journal and put two stars beside the entry. And I am afraid he has been eyeing the pile of parts that is Jeeves. Have I mentioned that Oliver never gives up on anyone?

Calypso is incorporating Wally's anti-mesmerism device into a line of fashion hats to be sold to the rich and powerful.

Even the Inn has changed. Now, if you linger in the lobby, you might notice *two* portraits over the mantel. One is of a stupid bird, but right beside it is a big-as-life portrait of President Theodore Roosevelt and . . .

. . . Wally!
Isn't he wonderful?

AUTHOR'S NOTE

SOME of my favorite authors—such as Isaac Asimov and Arthur C. Clarke—have been scientists as well as writers. It is not surprising that a scientist could be a great writer as well.

Both writers and scientists need good imaginations. Both need excellent problem-solving skills. Both enjoy reading and research. And both writers and scientists change things.

Writers change the people who live in the world.

Scientists change the world people live in.

Great writers and great scientists have two more things in common—they never stop learning and they never give up.

I hope that the Gadgets and Gears series inspires you to be both a great scientist and a great writer!

If you'd like to know more about the science and history in *The Mesmer Menace,* or want to exercise your imagination, ramp up your research, and polish your problem-solving skills, download the teacher's guide created by educator extraordinaire Christina Coppolillo:

www.scribd.com/doc/163972090/The-Mesmer-Menace-Teachers-Guide

About the Author
and Illustrator

Kersten Hamilton is the author of several picture books and many novels, including the critically acclaimed young adult trilogy the Goblin Wars. She has worked as a ranch hand, a woodcutter, a lumberjack, a census taker, a wrangler for wilderness guides and an archeological surveyor. Now, when she's not writing, she hunts dinosaurs in the deserts and badlands of New Mexico and tends to the animals on her farm in Kentucky. For more about Kersten, please visit www.kerstenhamilton.com.

James Hamilton is an artist and designer who lives in San Mateo, California. This is his first book.